ALISON MOORE has been writing stories since she was a child, and was first published – through a local writing competition – when she was eight. She began writing her first novel, *The Lighthouse*, the year her son was born, and has now had four novels published. *Sunny and the Ghosts* is her first book for children. She lives in a village on the Leicestershire-Nottinghamshire border with her husband and son and a cat called Shadow.

ROSS COLLINS was born in Glasgow, Scotland, quite a while ago. At that time he would eat anything and resembled a currant bun. Ross has written sixteen children's books and illustrated over a hundred. He no longer resembles a currant bun. He lives in Glasgow with a strange woman, a small child and a stupid dog.

SUNNY and the GHOSTS

Alison Moore

Illustrated by Ross Collins

SALT

CROMER

PUBLISHED BY SALT PUBLISHING 2018

2 4 6 8 10 9 7 5 3 1

First published in Great Britain in 2018 by
Salt Publishing Ltd
12 Norwich Road, Cromer, Norfolk NR27 0AX United Kingdom

www.saltpublishing.com

Salt Publishing Limited Reg. No. 5293401

A CIP catalogue record for this book is available from the British Library

ISBN 978 1 78463 126 0 (Paperback edition)
ISBN 978 1 78463 127 7 (Electronic edition)

Typeset in Neacademia by Salt Publishing

Printed and bound in Great Britain by Clays Ltd, Elcograf S.p.A

Salt Publishing Limited is committed to responsible forest management.
This book is made from Forest Stewardship Council™ certified paper.

For Arthur, Tommy and Tess

Sometimes, when you open a door or lift a lid, you find exactly what you expected to find: coats in the coat cupboard, bread in the bread bin, toys in the toy box. And sometimes you don't.

CHAPTER ONE

The First Ghost

I N THE NEW Year, Sunny's mum and dad bought a small shop in Devon, and the three of them moved into the flat above it. The shop sold antique furniture, vintage clothes, second-hand books. These were the words on the sign at the front of the shop –

Antique Vintage Second Hand

– and they all meant *old*. Everything in the shop was old, and sometimes what came into the shop was damaged, but between them they would fix it up and then Sunny's mum would say that it was as good as new. 'It's a funny phrase, that,' said Sunny's dad. 'Like new things are better than old things.'

Sunny's dad liked old things. When he went out in the van, as he had done just that morning to fetch a Victorian piano and a blanket box, he played golden oldies on the van's stereo – music from before Sunny was born, from before Sunny's dad was born, from when Sunny's grandparents were young. His dad said that these songs made the van feel happier. Sunny loved the old music, and he loved the old things that were brought back in the van.

His dad had once brought into the shop a wardrobe with an ancient winter coat hanging inside it. The coat's buttons were done up and the ends of the sleeves were tucked into the pockets as if someone invisible were still wearing it, still feeling the cold. 'I bet this coat could tell some stories,' he said to Sunny, taking it out of the wardrobe and hanging it up on a clothes rail on the far side of the shop. When his dad was not looking, Sunny put the coat back inside the wardrobe, where he felt it wanted to be.

His dad came home with mirrors that were more than a hundred years old. 'I bet this looking glass has seen a few things in its time,' he would say. It was Sunny's job to clean these mirrors which were hung on the wall, and to buff the brass coal scuttles that were displayed in the front window, and to polish the copper kettles, out of which he always felt – if he rubbed hard enough – a genie might appear.

He could get up such a shine that he could see his reflection in the pots and pans just as well as he could see it in a mirror. When his dad crouched down next to him to say, 'Great job, Sunny,' Sunny could see his dad's reflection too. The two of them had the same curly hair. Their hair just would not lie flat. It did what it wanted to do. It did its own thing.

Sunny's mum liked the old things too. She liked the butterflies, which had been preserved and labelled and framed like pictures. She liked the antique clocks, which were all set to the right time and once an hour all the ones that had cuckoos in them cuckooed and all the ones that bonged bonged. Against the wall on which the framed butterflies and the antique clocks hung, they placed the piano that had just arrived. Sunny's mum pressed down an ivory key and a deep note came out. 'Just think,' she said, 'how many tunes this piano must have played in its time.' One of these days, she said, she would learn to play the piano.

She especially loved a pair of ornamental pigs, which she put, very carefully, on top of the piano. The pigs were kind of weird but Sunny loved them too. They were round and shiny and he was tempted to play with them, but they were fragile and quite valuable and were the only items in the shop that Sunny was not allowed to touch, not even to clean them, in case they got broken.

Sunny polished the wooden furniture: the wardrobe,

the piano, the blanket box. He polished the wood until it looked like somebody loved it, like it was cared for. When he had finished, he opened up the blanket box. They had had a blanket box in the shop before. It had been full of blankets. Inside this one, he found a ghost.

'Dad . . . ?' he called, but his dad was in the back of the van, moving things around, and could not hear him.

'Mum . . . ?' he called, but his mum was upstairs with the radio on and could not hear him.

Sunny stared at the ghost, who looked very old and wore stripy pyjamas. He looked gaunt and unhappy and was moaning and groaning. Even after he got out of the blanket box and could stretch out his thin limbs, he still seemed unhappy.

'What's wrong?' asked Sunny.

'I feel travel sick,' said the ghost.

Sunny tried to rub the ghost's back, and fetched him a drink of water. The ghost said thank you and lifted the glass to his ghostly mouth, but the water fell straight through his ghostly body and made a puddle on the floor.

'Oh dear,' said the ghost. 'I'm very sorry.'

'Don't worry,' said Sunny, and he fetched a cloth and mopped up the puddle. 'What are you doing here?' he asked.

'I was brought here in the blanket box,' said the ghost.

4

'But what were you doing in the blanket box?' asked Sunny.

'I was frightened,' said the ghost. 'For days, I'd been alone and everything had been quiet, and then all of a sudden I heard people. I was in my bedroom and I could hear men talking and making a lot of noise in the hallway and then coming up the stairs. I hid in the blanket box. It's nice in there, very cosy. But then I felt it being picked up and carried out of the house. It was put into the back of the van, along with the piano, and I was brought here.'

'That will have been my dad,' said Sunny.

'What will?' said his dad, coming back into the shop with a coat stand and a teapot.

'Dad,' said Sunny, 'there was a ghost in the blanket box.'

'Was there now?' said his dad. 'Well, that is unusual. I imagine it will feel right at home here though, amongst all these old things.' He put down the coat stand and the teapot. 'Right, that's enough for today, let's go up and have our tea.' Sunny turned around to ask the ghost if he would be all right and if he needed anything, but the ghost had gone.

In his bedroom above the shop, in the middle of the night, Sunny woke up. He could hear music, piano music. He lay in his bed, listening. It was coming from downstairs.

He picked up his night light, got out of bed and went to his parents' room. When he opened the door, his mum woke up, and Sunny said, 'Mum, I can hear someone playing the piano in the shop.'

His mum sat up and listened. 'I can't hear anyone playing the piano,' she said. And neither could Sunny now – the house was silent. 'You must have been dreaming,' said his mum. 'Go back to bed.'

Sunny went back to bed, but no sooner had he got back under the covers than the piano music started again. He got out of bed and took his night light back out onto the landing. He could definitely hear music down there in the dark. He pushed open his parents' bedroom door and the music stopped. His dad sat up. 'Dad,' said Sunny, 'I heard someone playing the piano in the shop.'

'I didn't hear anything,' said his dad, but he was listening really hard, like he wasn't sure.

'Can we go and look?' asked Sunny.

His dad sighed. 'All right,' he said. He found his slippers and rubbed his eyes. 'Let's go and see.'

His dad switched on the landing light and went down first, his feet heavy on the stairs. He switched on the hallway light and said, 'Let's have a look then,' as he opened the door to the shop and went in. In the light from the hallway and from the streetlamp at the front of the shop, Sunny, looking at the piano, saw the evidence straight away.

'Look,' he said, 'the lid of the piano's up.'

'You must have left it up after giving it a polish,' said his dad, putting the lid down again.

'I didn't,' said Sunny. 'It must have been the ghost.'

His dad rubbed his face and said, 'Come on, back to bed.' He shut the door behind them, and switched off the hallway light, and then the landing light, and they both went back to bed.

Sunny lay under the covers, listening, until he finally fell asleep, just as the first few notes of *Bananas in Pyjamas* were coming up the stairs.

From Monday to Saturday, the shop opened at nine o'clock in the morning and closed at five o'clock in the afternoon. There was a sign on the door that said so:

OPEN
Monday to Saturday
9am to 5pm

At five o'clock, the sign was turned around so that it said CLOSED, and the front door was locked, and then it was teatime. Except that there was one regular customer, Mr Ramsbottom, who was in the habit of coming into the shop at one minute to five, as he did one Saturday when Sunny was in the shop with his dad. Mr Ramsbottom came in eating a jam doughnut in spite of another sign that said NO FOOD OR DRINK IN THE SHOP. It even said PLEASE *and* THANK YOU.

'I'm afraid we're closing in a minute,' said Sunny's dad, who had at that very moment been fetching the door key from the cash desk.

Mr Ramsbottom walked slowly around the shop. He looked at the cuckoo clocks, and at the cuckoo-ing cuckoos. He opened and closed the lid of the piano. He picked up every copper kettle and every brass pot. He inspected a glass fruit bowl and took out a couple of the plastic apples displayed inside it. Since retiring, Mr Ramsbottom had been finding new hobbies to fill his time. He had been learning to play the violin, and he had been learning to juggle. Sunny had seen him practising, juggling oranges and tomatoes outside the greengrocer's. He had seen the fruit landing in the gutter, and Mr Ramsbottom refusing to buy it.

'Mr Ramsbottom . . .' said Sunny's dad, but Mr Ramsbottom was busy juggling the plastic apples. Sunny's dad said again, 'Mr Ramsbottom . . .'

'Don't put me off,' said Mr Ramsbottom. He struggled to juggle more than two things at a time – if he tried to add a third orange or tomato or plastic apple, he was likely to drop the lot. Luckily, the plastic apples did not burst when dropped, unlike the tomatoes.

At ten past five, Sunny's dad said, 'I'm afraid I'll have to lock up soon.'

When Mr Ramsbottom had gone all the way around the shop once, he went back around the shop for a second look at everything.

At twenty past five, Sunny's dad said, 'We'll be open again at nine o'clock on Monday morning, Mr Ramsbottom.'

Mr Ramsbottom continued to browse. Sunny could smell the sausages that he knew they were having for

tea and which were probably already on the table. His tummy rumbled, and then he heard his dad's tummy rumbling too.

At half past five, Sunny's dad said to Mr Ramsbottom, 'Are you looking for anything in particular?'

'No,' said Mr Ramsbottom. 'I don't want anything you've got in this shop.' And, leaving the kettles and pots and pans all out of place and in need of another polish, Mr Ramsbottom left.

Sunday was the one day of the week when the shop was closed to the public, but Sunny was often in there helping out.

'Right, Sunny,' said his dad, coming up from the cellar with a cardboard box full of old books. 'I've got a job for you.' He put down the box. 'Mr Ramsbottom's sister has moved to America. These were her books but she decided not to take them with her. She left them with Mr Ramsbottom, but he doesn't want them so he's sold them to us.'

Sunny looked at his dad. They both knew that when Mr Ramsbottom sold them something, he was likely to change his mind about it later and want it back. At one time or another, he had been in with a gramophone with a broken turntable, and a grandfather clock that was not keeping time, and all sorts of other things, which Sunny's dad had fixed and which Sunny had polished, and then Mr Ramsbottom had come into the shop saying that, as a matter of fact, he wanted his things back. Sunny's dad always returned Mr Ramsbottom's things without complaining and without charging him for the time spent fixing them up, but whenever he saw Mr Ramsbottom coming he sighed.

Sunny's dad pointed to the box of books. 'These books,' he said, 'need to go on those shelves.' He pointed to a bookcase. 'Put them alphabetically: Adams, Brontë, Carroll, Dickens, and so on.'

While his dad went off to make a cup of tea, Sunny knelt down in front of the bookcase and started putting the books in order on the shelves. He had just got to Dickens when he heard someone moaning.

'I'm *so bored*,' said this whingeing voice.

Sunny looked around and saw the ghost that had been in the blanket box. 'Why don't you play the piano?' suggested Sunny, putting *A Christmas Carol* on a bookshelf.

'I can't,' said the ghost. 'I don't know how to.'

'But I heard you,' said Sunny. 'I heard you playing

in the middle of the night. You play very well.'

'That wasn't me,' said the ghost. 'I've never played a note. I don't know any tunes.'

'But I thought it was your piano,' said Sunny. 'I mean, it came from the same house as the blanket box that you were inside.'

'It *is* my piano,' said the ghost, 'it belonged to my mother – but I never learnt to play it.'

'Oh,' said Sunny. 'Well, if it wasn't you playing, who was it?'

'That was Walter,' said the ghost, and while Sunny finished shelving the books, the ghost moaned about Walter. 'He played the piano all night long,' said the ghost. 'He played *Bananas in Pyjamas* over and over again, I don't know how many times, I lost count.'

'Where's Walter now?' asked Sunny.

'He's in the wardrobe,' said the ghost, nodding to the wardrobe that had the winter coat inside it. Sunny went over to the wardrobe and opened the doors, but all he could see in there was the coat hanging from the rail.

His dad came back into the shop and saw Sunny standing by the wardrobe. 'Have you done the books?' he said. 'Good lad.'

'Dad,' said Sunny, 'I think there's a ghost in this wardrobe.'

'Do you now?' said his dad.

'His name's Walter,' said Sunny.

'And what makes you think there's a ghost in the wardrobe?' asked his dad.

'The other ghost told me,' said Sunny, turning towards where the ghost had been, but it was no longer there. 'The one that was in the blanket box.'

'And what's *his* name?' asked his dad.

'I don't know,' said Sunny.

His dad shook his head, and frowned at the coat in the wardrobe. He lifted it out on its hanger and hung it instead on the clothes rail on the far side of the shop.

Sunny's mum's voice came down the stairs: 'Tea's ready!' she called.

'Come on then, Sunny,' said his dad. 'Teatime.'

Sunny waited until his dad was on the stairs and then moved the coat back into the wardrobe, where he felt it belonged.

On his way out of the shop, he stopped at the blanket box, lifted the lid and found the ghost inside. 'What's your name?' he asked.

'Herbert,' said the ghost.

'I've got to go now, Herbert,' said Sunny. 'It's time for my tea.'

'Is it the end of the day already?' asked Herbert. He pulled a miserable face. 'Now Walter will start playing the piano again, I know he will, and I'll have to listen, all night long, just like last night.'

'Couldn't you sleep last night?' asked Sunny.

'No,' said Herbert.

'When I can't sleep, I count,' said Sunny. 'You could try counting.'

'What should I count?' asked Herbert.

'Anything you like,' said Sunny. 'Sheep, green bottles . . .'

'Bananas in pyjamas . . .' said Herbert.

'Bananas in pyjamas . . .' said Sunny.

'All right,' said Herbert. He closed his eyes. 'One banana in pyjamas, two bananas in pyjamas, three bananas in pyjamas . . .'

Sunny closed the lid of the blanket box and went upstairs for his tea.

CHAPTER TWO

The Second Ghost

O N MONDAY, SUNNY'S dad went out early and came back before breakfast with a vanload of rather fine things. There was a crystal chandelier, a silk rug, and a leather trunk which Sunny's mum admired. She opened the lid of the trunk, looked inside, and closed it again. 'We should put it near the window,' she said, 'where someone's more likely to see it and want to buy it.' They moved the blanket box aside to make space for the handsome trunk, in front of which they placed the rug and above which they hung the chandelier.

While Sunny was at school, he kept thinking about the ghosts. He told his friends about them, but his friends said that ghosts were not real, that they were only in stories.

'But I saw one,' said Sunny. 'He's living in a blanket box in the shop. His name's Herbert.'

17

His friends looked doubtful. They were so doubtful that Sunny started doubting it himself. Perhaps, he thought, he had only dreamt it, or had just imagined it. He wanted to go and look inside the blanket box again, to see if Herbert was there. But after school, Sunny had football club, and as soon as he got home it was time for tea.

He was in the kitchen, getting three sets of cutlery out of the cutlery drawer, when his dad came in.

'That box of books I gave you yesterday,' said his dad. 'I thought you'd put them in the bookcase. You were supposed to put them on the shelves.'

'I did,' said Sunny.

'Well,' said his dad, 'when I looked this morning, they were all over the shop. Two of the Shakespeares were on top of the piano. I found one of the Brontës down the back of the chaise longue. Nothing was in the right place. And I can't find A *Christmas Carol* anywhere.'

'I put the books on the shelves,' said Sunny. 'I put them in alphabetical order.'

'Well, then,' said his dad, 'it must have been those ghosts of yours.'

'What ghosts?' asked Sunny's mum, bringing a big dish of spaghetti to the table.

They all sat down and Sunny's dad said, 'There

are ghosts in the shop. They're in the furniture, aren't they, Sunny?'

'Yes,' said Sunny.

'Oh, I see,' said his mum, spooning spaghetti onto Sunny's plate. 'Is that who was playing the piano on Saturday night?'

'Yes,' said Sunny.

'He lives in the blanket box,' said Sunny's dad. 'His name's Walter.'

'No,' said Sunny. 'That's Herbert in the blanket box. Walter's in the wardrobe, but I haven't seen him yet.'

After tea, it was bathtime, and then bedtime, and Sunny was so tired he fell asleep in the middle of a chapter of his book. But during the night, he woke up. He could hear the piano music again. He got out of bed and crept out of his room. He had his night light with him and left the landing light off. He went down the stairs as quietly as he possibly could. When he opened the door to the shop, he found, sitting on the piano stool, a ghost, which looked up at him in surprise. It was not the ghost from the blanket box;

it was another one, a younger man, smartly dressed in not just a shirt and trousers but also a waistcoat with the chain of a pocket watch showing.

'Are you Walter?' asked Sunny.

'Yes,' said the ghost.

'Where's Herbert?' asked Sunny.

'He's in the blanket box,' said Walter. 'He's counting.'

Sunny went to the blanket box and lifted the lid.

'Ninety nine thousand, eight hundred and fifty *four* bananas in pyjamas,' said Herbert, 'ninety nine thousand, eight hundred and fifty *five* bananas in pyjamas . . .'

'Didn't counting help you sleep?' asked Sunny.

'No,' said Herbert with a sigh. 'I don't think ghosts *can* sleep.'

'Herbert, Walter,' said Sunny, 'do you know why the books were all over the shop? Yesterday, I put them on the bookshelves, but this morning my dad found *Hamlet* and *Macbeth* on top of the piano, and one of the Brontës down the back of the chaise longue.'

'It wasn't me,' said Walter.

'It wasn't me,' said Herbert. 'Which Brontë is it?'

'*Wuthering Heights*,' said Sunny.

'Really?' said Herbert, climbing out of the blanket box. 'That's my favourite.'

'It's back in the bookcase now,' said Sunny. 'You

can read it if you like, as long as you put it back on the shelf when you've finished with it. We can't find *A Christmas Carol* anywhere.' To Walter, he said, 'You play the piano very well.'

'Thank you,' said Walter. He looked pleased but a bit shy. 'I think I'll get back in the wardrobe now.' He left the piano stool and went back to the wardrobe, slipping into the winter coat, settling down inside it so that Sunny could not see Walter's head, not even his tufty hair.

'Are you all right in there?' asked Sunny. He heard Walter's muffled but cheerful reply. 'Night night, Walter,' said Sunny, closing the wardrobe door. 'Night night, Herbert.'

Herbert was sitting by the window now, reading the first page of *Wuthering Heights* by moonlight. 'Night night, Sunny,' said Herbert. 'Have a nice sleep.'

Every day that week, Sunny woke up wondering if it was Saturday yet. He wanted to spend some time with the ghosts. He wondered how they were doing and what they were getting up to.

On Wednesday, at teatime, Sunny's dad said, 'One

of the ornamental pigs is missing. Do you know where it is?'

'No,' said Sunny.

'You would say, wouldn't you, if maybe you'd cleaned it and broken it by accident?' said his mum.

'I haven't touched it,' said Sunny. 'I'll see if the ghosts know anything about it.'

'Did they own up to scattering those books?' asked his dad.

'Walter said it wasn't him,' said Sunny, 'and Herbert said it wasn't him, but I did tell Herbert he could read the books as long as he puts them back on the shelves when he's finished with them.'

'Well,' said his dad, 'just as long as he does. I don't know how they got into such a mess.'

'It's a mystery,' said Sunny's mum.

'Yes,' said Sunny's dad. 'It's a mystery.'

A little after midnight, Sunny was once again woken by the piano music. He reached for his night light and went downstairs and into the shop. Walter was at the piano, on top of which there was now only one pig. Herbert was by the window, reading. Sunny said to the ghosts, 'One of the pigs is missing. Do you know where it is?'

'No,' said Walter. 'I haven't touched it.'

'Me neither,' said Herbert. 'It's bound to turn up though. It won't be far away.'

Sunny yawned and wished the ghosts goodnight, and while he was climbing the stairs, Walter played a lullaby.

The following morning, while Sunny was getting ready for school, his dad went down to the shop. A minute later, he came back upstairs and said, 'It's full of cats.'

'What's full of cats?' asked Sunny's mum.

'The shop,' said Sunny's dad. 'It's full of cats.'

They all went together down to the shop, which was full of cats. There were dozens of them: black ones, white ones, black and white ones, grey ones, ginger ones, tabby ones, big ones, little ones, fat ones, skinny ones; they were sleeping on cushions and table-tops and shelves, and on the windowsills, in amongst the pots and pans, and *in* the pots and pans; or they were wandering around, jumping up, jumping down,

batting things, chasing things, chasing their own tails round in circles; they purred and miaowed and yowled.

'How did all these cats get in?' asked Sunny's mum.

'I don't know,' said Sunny's dad. 'The door's locked, and the key's right where it ought to be.' He went to fetch the key and opened the door, and they herded the cats out, waking the ones that were sleeping, finding them in all sorts of unexpected places. The very last one was found in the leather trunk.

At school, Sunny told his friends about the shop being full of cats.

'First it was ghosts,' said his friend Ellie, 'and now it's cats.'

'It's both,' said Sunny.

'I'll stop off at the shop on the way home from school,' said Ellie. 'I'd like to see the cats.'

'Well,' said Sunny, 'they've all gone now.'

'What about the ghosts?' asked Ellie.

'They're still there,' said Sunny.

After school, Ellie walked home with Sunny. They went in through the front door, into the shop. 'Look in there,' said Sunny, pointing to the blanket box.

'Has it got ghosts in it?' asked Ellie, walking over to the blanket box.

'It's got *a* ghost in it,' said Sunny.

Ellie lifted the lid and looked inside. 'Wow,' she said.

'See?' said Sunny.

'There are dozens of them,' said Ellie. 'Fat ones, skinny ones, some sleeping, some running around, chasing their tails . . .'

'What?' said Sunny. He went over, took hold of the lid and looked inside the box. Herbert wasn't in there; the blanket box was empty.

'I'll see you tomorrow,' said Ellie, heading for the front door, going home.

Sunny was still standing there, holding the lid of the blanket box, when he heard the wardrobe door creaking open behind him. He looked, and saw Herbert coming out of the wardrobe.

'What were you doing in there?' Sunny asked him.

'Walter invited me over to his place for the afternoon,' said Herbert.

'I wanted you to meet my friend Ellie,' said Sunny.

'Well, I am popular today, aren't I?' said Herbert, and his ghostly face looked very pleased. 'I'll be needing a calendar,' he said, 'to keep track of all my appointments.'

Finally, Saturday came, when Sunny could spend the day helping out in the shop. Sunny and his mum were sitting at the kitchen table, starting on their breakfast, while Sunny's dad was on the phone in the hallway. Sunny saw him go down to the shop, and he heard what sounded like every note on the piano being played, from the deepest note at one end of the keyboard to the highest note at the other end. Sunny's dad came back upstairs and into the kitchen and said, 'Mr Ramsbottom wants to buy the piano.'

'No!' said Sunny. 'Walter *loves* playing the piano.'

Sunny's dad sat down at the table, and his face settled into a frown. 'I just went down to take a look at it,' he said, 'and while I was down there I found the other pig.'

'Oh good!' said Sunny's mum.

'I found it on the floor,' said Sunny's dad, 'broken into pieces.'

'Oh no!' said Sunny's mum.

Sunny realised that both his mum and his dad were looking at him. 'It wasn't me!' said Sunny. 'I didn't touch it!'

'No,' said his dad. 'I didn't see the breakage when I locked up yesterday, so I know it can't have been you, unless you're in the habit of wandering around the shop in the middle of the night.'

Sunny's mouth was full of toast, so he didn't say anything; he didn't mention that he did sometimes go down to the shop in the middle of the night to talk to the ghosts.

'But how did it happen?' said his dad. 'It wasn't me, and it wasn't you,' he said to Sunny's mum, 'and it wasn't Sunny. Who can have done it?'

Sunny, who had swallowed his toast now, said, 'It won't have been Herbert or Walter.'

'Maybe another cat got in,' said Sunny's mum.

'But it wasn't there to get knocked over by a cat or anything else,' said Sunny's dad. 'It's been missing since Wednesday.'

'It's a mystery,' said Sunny's mum.

'Yes,' said Sunny's dad. 'It's a mystery.'

When they got down to the shop, Sunny saw the pig lying on the floor in at least half a dozen pieces. His dad picked the pieces up very carefully and went to put them somewhere safe for gluing back together. While his dad was out of the shop, Sunny went to the wardrobe and said to the winter coat, 'Somebody wants to buy the piano.'

A big *ohhh* came out of the coat. 'But I *love* playing the piano,' said Walter. 'Now I'll have nothing to do.'

'You can read the books,' said Sunny. 'We've got lots of good books.'

'But I can't read,' said Walter. 'I never learnt. I didn't go to school.'

'You didn't go to school?' said Sunny. 'Not ever?'

'No,' said Walter. 'When I was five years old, about two hundred years ago, I started working in the pit.'

'In a coal mine?' said Sunny.

'Aye,' said Walter. 'I worked there all my life. I always wanted to learn to read, but I never did.'

Just then, there was a banging at the door of the shop, and Sunny turned to see what the noise was. He saw Mr Ramsbottom standing there, hammering his fist against the glass door. Sunny looked at the time – it was only half past eight. His dad came into the shop and sighed. 'All right, all right,' he said, going to the door and opening up for Mr Ramsbottom.

'You've got to unlock the door if you want to sell anything,' said Mr Ramsbottom. 'You can't keep a customer waiting out in the cold like that.'

'We don't open until nine o'clock,' said Sunny's dad.

Mr Ramsbottom came inside, pushing past Sunny's

dad, who closed the door behind him. The two men went over to the piano.

'It's very old,' said Mr Ramsbottom.

'It's an antique,' said Sunny's dad. 'It's in excellent condition.'

Mr Ramsbottom grumbled about the price, but he paid and Sunny's dad said that he would bring it round in the van later that morning.

While Sunny's dad was phoning someone who would help him to move the piano, Sunny opened the blanket box and said to the ghost, 'Herbert, the pig turned up but it's been broken.'

'It wasn't me!' said Herbert.

'It wasn't me!' said Walter, who was listening through the wardrobe door.

'It's a mystery,' said Sunny.

While Sunny's dad was busy getting the piano into the van, Sunny's mum came downstairs to mind the shop.

'Mum,' said Sunny, 'please can I get something out of the stationery cupboard?'

The stationery cupboard was a big, walk-in cupboard in which they kept the shop's supply of paper and envelopes and so on, but there was more in there than just stationery. The stationery cupboard was also where they kept a vacuum cleaner, and polish and dusters, and Sunny's drawing and painting things for when he felt like drawing or painting, and there was packaging, like rolls of bubblewrap and empty boxes.

'Of course you can,' said his mum, taking the key out of the drawer of the cash desk. 'What do you need to get from the cupboard? Are you going to do some drawing?'

'I need a box,' said Sunny.

'A box? An empty box?' said his mum.

'Yes,' said Sunny. 'Please.'

'What do you need a box for?' asked his mum.

'I want to teach Walter to read,' said Sunny.

His mum gave him a curious look, but she unlocked the door to the stationery cupboard. The empty boxes were up on the highest shelf. She got one down and gave it to Sunny. 'OK?' she said.

'Yes,' said Sunny. 'Thanks.'

His mum was straightening the remaining boxes before locking the cupboard, and Sunny was walking back through the shop, when Walter stuck his head out of the wardrobe door and said, 'You want to teach me to read?'

'Yes,' said Sunny. 'Do you want to try?'

'All right,' said Walter.

'Wait there,' said Sunny.

'I'm not going anywhere,' said Walter.

Sunny went upstairs to his bedroom and returned with a box full of books. He took it over to the chaise longue, which was in a quiet alcove, away from the front door and out of sight of the cash desk. He sat down, and Walter perched beside him, looking at the books. Walter reached out and touched one, very gently, as if it were sleeping and about to be woken up. 'Let's try this one,' he said.

'All right,' said Sunny, taking it out and opening it up. 'This one's really good.'

While Sunny's mum flipped the sign on the shop door, so that it now said OPEN, Sunny and Walter got started.

Walter said, 'It'll be a while before I'm reading Shakespeare.'

'That's OK,' said Sunny. 'You've got all the time in the world.'

CHAPTER THREE

The Third Ghost

R ATTLE-RATTLE-RATTLE.

Sunny, who was just getting another book out of the box for Walter, looked up.

Rattle-rattle-rattle.

The sound was coming from the stationery cupboard.

Rattle-rattle-rattle.

It was the handle of the stationery cupboard door, jiggling noisily, being noisily jiggled, although Sunny could not see who was doing the jiggling. Perhaps it was being jiggled from the inside.

He knew that his mum was not in there, because she was in the back room on the other side of the shop, making a cup of tea. Sunny walked over to the stationery cupboard. He reached for the handle – he thought that the door was locked, but he checked anyway. He turned the handle and pulled, and pulled again, but the door was definitely locked.

'Hello?' he said, through the door, but there was no reply. He bent down to the keyhole and looked through. He said again, through the keyhole, 'Hello?'

'Who are you talking to?' asked his mum, coming back into the shop with her cup of tea.

'I think there's somebody locked in the stationery cupboard,' said Sunny. He watched the door handle, but it was not jiggling or rattling now.

'That would be very odd,' said his mum. 'There's no one in the shop but you and me, and it's not either of us in there.' She knocked on the door, as if it were the door to someone's house, and said, 'Hello?' but there was no answer. She went to the cash desk and came back with the key. 'Stand back,' she said to Sunny, as if there might be something terrible like a fire-breathing dragon in there, one that could jiggle a door handle. She unlocked the stationery cupboard door and opened it wide. Sunny saw exactly what he expected to see inside the stationery cupboard: paper and envelopes, rolls of bubblewrap and empty boxes, the vacuum cleaner and so on, and a ghost. Her ghostly hair was frizzy – as if an awful lot of electricity had gone through it – and she had a startled look on her ghostly face.

'Well,' said Sunny's mum, 'there's no one in there.'

'Can't you see anyone?' asked Sunny.

'No one at all,' said Sunny's mum. 'It must have been your imagination.'

The ghost came out of the cupboard, edging past Sunny's mum, who closed and locked the cupboard door and put the key back into the drawer of the cash desk. At that moment, the phone in the hallway rang and Sunny's mum went to answer it. Sunny heard her speaking to the person on the other end of the line. He heard her say, 'A pig? Well, bring it in.'

Sunny turned to the ghost. 'Hello,' he said.

'Hello,' said the ghost. 'Gosh, I thought I was never going to get out of there. I was trying the handle but the door wouldn't open. Then I heard a voice coming through the door and through the keyhole, and the handle started moving – jiggling and rattling – and there was this knocking . . . I didn't know who was doing it, it was spooky, I was getting scared.'

'It was just me, and my mum. I'm Sunny.'

'I'm Violet,' said the ghost.

'How come you were stuck in the stationery cupboard?' asked Sunny. 'Can't you walk through doors?'

'No,' said Violet. 'Can you?'

Herbert had come out of his blanket box now. He came over and said hello to the new ghost, and Sunny explained about Violet having been stuck in the

stationery cupboard. 'Can *you* walk through doors?' he said to Herbert and Walter.

'It's easier if the door is *open*,' said Walter. 'Going through a closed door is very uncomfortable, and I can't do it when I'm tired.'

'I don't know if I can or not,' said Herbert. 'Shall I try? I'll try getting out of the cupboard.'

'All right,' said Sunny. He went to fetch the key and opened the cupboard door again. Herbert went inside and closed the door behind him. There was a pause, and then they heard a bump against the door, and then another one. The door opened and Herbert came out rubbing his head.

'No,' said Herbert. 'No, I can't.'

'I think it's something you have to learn how to do,' said Walter.

'Like whistling,' said Sunny. His dad whistled while he worked, and Sunny would have liked to do the same. When he was six he thought that when he was seven he'd be able to whistle; when he was seven he thought that when he was eight he'd be able to whistle; and now he was eight he was hoping that when he was nine he'd be able to whistle. He could understand how a ghost might find it difficult to walk through a door.

He said to Violet, 'What were you doing in the stationery cupboard?'

'I went in there looking for some paper,' she said.

'Notepaper?' asked Sunny. 'For writing a letter?'

'I want to write a book,' said Violet. 'I always thought I'd like to try writing one, but I never got around to it.'

'Shall I see if you're allowed to use the computer?' asked Sunny, but Violet said she would rather use a pen.

'Or a typewriter,' she said, looking at a small collection of old typewriters at the back of the shop, 'but that might be a bit noisy.'

Sunny thought about the piano music that had been waking him up at night, and said yes, it might be a bit noisy.

'A pen will be fine,' said Violet. 'And some paper. And lots and lots of time.'

'You could sit at the cash desk,' said Sunny, 'although someone's usually sitting there during the day.'

'I think I'd like to rest in the stationery cupboard during the day,' said Violet. 'In the daytime, people tend to walk through me, or sit right where I'm sitting, and I don't like the way it feels.'

Sunny understood this – he had once accidentally put his hand through Herbert, and it had looked very uncomfortable.

'At night,' said Violet, 'I'll write at the desk.'

'And when you've finished writing your book,' said Walter, 'perhaps I'll be able to read it.'

At the end of the day, when the shop was shut – when the door had been locked and the sign had been turned from OPEN to CLOSED – Sunny let Violet out of the stationery cupboard and she settled down to write at the desk. 'Do you know,' she said, 'I don't really know how I came to be here.'

'In the shop?' asked Herbert, climbing out of the blanket box.

'No, I came into the shop inside a box of books,' said Violet, 'although I'm not sure where it's gone now. I mean, I don't really know how I came to be in the afterlife.'

'Well, what's the last thing you remember?' asked Herbert.

'I was just making toast,' said Violet, 'to go with a boiled egg.' She thought for a moment. 'I remember the toast being stuck in the toaster, so I was poking a fork into the slot to try and get it out.'

'Ah,' said Herbert. 'You should never do that, it's very dangerous.'

'Yes,' said Violet, 'I'll remember that.' After a moment, she said to him, 'What's the last thing *you* remember?'

'I had a new bag of gobstoppers,' said Herbert.

'They were really big ones, and I thought to myself, I wonder how many I could fit in my mouth in one go. I remember squeezing in number six.'

'I expect you wish,' said Violet, 'that you'd eaten them one at a time and made them last.'

'Yes,' said Herbert longingly.

On Monday morning, Sunny woke up to the sound of feet banging up the stairs. He heard his mum say, 'What? No, it's . . .'

'But look!' said his dad. 'Come and look!'

Sunny heard two pairs of feet thudding down the stairs. He came out of his bedroom and went down to the shop, where his dad was gesticulating towards the clock that hung above the cash desk. The little hand was pointing to the nine and the big hand was pointing straight up. 'And look . . .' said his dad, drawing their attention to the other clocks – the antique clocks hanging on the wall above the space where the piano had been – which one by one were striking nine o'clock: there was a CUCKOO! and then a BONG! and another CUCKOO! and another BONG! and then all the clocks that cuckooed were cuckooing and all the ones that bonged were bonging and Sunny said, 'It's nine o'clock! I'm late for school!' He was supposed to be at school right now – he was supposed to be in assembly – and he was still in his pyjamas. One by one, the clocks were all ticking on to one minute past nine. The shop was supposed to be open already, and there indeed was Mr Ramsbottom, at the front door, peering through the glass. Sunny's dad, who was also still wearing pyjamas, went to open up. 'I'm so sorry,' he said. 'Do come in.' He turned the shop sign from CLOSED to OPEN.

Mr Ramsbottom gave him a funny look as he came in.

Sunny's mum said to Sunny's dad, 'But it's not nine o'clock yet.'

'It is,' said Sunny's dad. 'Look at the clocks.'

'The clocks are wrong,' said Sunny's mum.

'They can't be wrong,' said Sunny's dad. 'They can't *all* be wrong.'

Mr Ramsbottom had sat down on the chaise longue and was bouncing up and down, testing the springs. 'They *are* wrong,' he said. 'It's only seven thirty.'

'But . . .' said Sunny's dad, staring up at the clocks. 'But . . .'

'It's only seven thirty,' said Sunny's mum, showing him the time on her wristwatch.

'But why were you at the door so early, Mr Ramsbottom?' asked Sunny's dad.

'Oh, I was just walking past on my way to buy milk for my breakfast,' said Mr Ramsbottom. 'I saw you all standing in here in your pyjamas so I had a good look through the window. You opened the door so I came in for a sit down.'

'But why are the clocks all telling the wrong time?' asked Sunny's dad, gazing at them in bafflement.

'It's a mystery,' said Mr Ramsbottom.

Sunny's mum helped Mr Ramsbottom to his feet. 'Off you go, then, Mr Ramsbottom,' she said. 'You can go and get your milk now.' She locked the door behind him and turned the shop sign from OPEN to CLOSED again. 'And let's go and get our breakfast as well,' she said to Sunny and his dad.

Just as Sunny was going into the hallway, he heard some kind of sound behind them, in the shop, and then his dad pulled the door to. It had been – thought Sunny, as he was going up the stairs – a kind of squeaky, creaky sound. It had been – he thought, when he was sitting in the kitchen, eating his toast – a bit like the sound of a wheezy chuckle.

CHAPTER FOUR

The Fourth Ghost, and the Fifth

ONE DAY, SUNNY'S dad took the van all the way to London. He left first thing in the morning and did not get home until the evening, when Sunny was getting ready for bed. But the next day was Saturday, and when Sunny walked into the shop, the first thing he saw was a rocking chair that had not been there before, so it must have come all the way from London; and, in the rocking chair, there was a ghost. She had long ghostly hair and wore a long ghostly nightdress. Sunny went over to her. 'Hello,' he said, 'welcome to our shop.'

'Thank you very much,' said the ghost.

'Who are you talking to?' asked his mum, coming into the shop with her arms full of old clothes for mending.

'A ghost,' said Sunny.

'Ah,' said his mum. 'The one who plays the piano.'

'No,' said Sunny, 'not that one. There's another one—'

'The one who lives in the blanket box,' said his mum.

'No,' said Sunny. 'It's another one, a new one.'

'Ah,' said his mum, and went out again.

Sunny turned back to the ghost in the rocking chair and said, 'I'm Sunny.'

'Pleased to meet you,' said the ghost. 'I'm Miss Constantine.'

'Have you met Herbert?' asked Sunny, going over to the blanket box, but when he opened it up, Herbert wasn't in there. Then he heard him, in the hallway at the back of the shop, and there he was, coming in from the garden.

'I was just showing our new guest around the garden,' said Herbert, and there was Miss Constantine, coming in behind him.

'How did you get there?' asked Sunny, turning to look at the rocking chair again, but Miss Constantine was there too, still in the rocking chair *and* coming down the hallway behind Herbert.

'This is Miss Constantine,' said Herbert.

'Yes,' said Sunny, eyeing this Miss Constantine who was walking down the hallway towards him, and then

turning again to look at the Miss Constantine who was rocking in the rocking chair. 'We've met. But how is she . . . Why are there . . .'

'Miss Constantine,' said Herbert, taking the arm of the ghost he had shown around the garden, 'and Miss Constantine,' he said, gesturing towards the ghost in the rocking chair, 'are twin sisters. This is Miss Elsie Constantine.' Elsie was the one who had been into the garden. She had the same long ghostly hair and wore the same long ghostly nightdress as her sister. 'And this is Miss Mary Constantine.' Mary was the one who was sitting in the rocking chair.

'You can just call us Mary and Elsie,' said Mary.

'Thank you, Mary,' said Sunny. 'And I'm pleased to meet you, Elsie. Have you come all the way from London?'

'We have,' said Elsie. 'We've been in our house in London for a very long time. Then men came for the furniture, and we looked out of the window and saw their vehicle, and on the side it gave the name of your shop and the address – an address in Devon, and we know that's where the seaside is. Well, we always wanted to see the sea, but we've never been. So we made sure that when the furniture went into the vehicle, we went in too, and here we are.'

'But we don't live by the sea,' said Sunny. 'We do live in Devon but we're miles away from the sea.'

Elsie and Mary looked disappointed, so Sunny said, 'But maybe we could go. We could go on a day trip to the seaside.'

'Oooh!' said Elsie, and, 'Oooh!' said Mary, and they sounded just like the ghosts in Sunny's storybooks.

'Can I come too?' asked Herbert.

'And me?' asked Walter, poking his head out of the wardrobe.

'And me?' asked Violet, through the stationery cupboard door.

'I'll have to ask my mum and dad,' said Sunny.

'Ask us what?' said his mum, coming back into the shop with her sewing kit.

'The ghosts want to go to the seaside,' said Sunny.

'Are you trying to say,' said his mum, 'that *you* would like to go to the seaside?'

'Yes,' said Sunny.

'All right,' said his mum. 'We can go one Sunday, when the shop's closed. We'll all go: you and me and your dad.'

'And the ghosts,' said Sunny.

'And the ghosts,' said his mum. 'Of course.'

'I'm rather tired,' said Elsie, 'after that walk around the garden.'

'Take a turn in the rocking chair, dear,' said Mary, standing up.

'Thank you, dear,' said Elsie, sitting down.

Herbert said to Mary, 'Would you like to see the garden?'

'Thank you,' said Mary, 'I would,' and they headed for the hallway.

Meanwhile, Elsie sat rocking in the rocking chair. Sunny's mum watched the chair creaking to and fro on the floorboards. She frowned and scratched her head. Then the door at the far end of the hallway opened and the cold air came in. Sunny's mum turned her head. The door closed again. 'Ah,' she said, 'the back door's blowing open and shut – the draught must be what's making this chair move.'

'It's not a draught,' said Sunny, 'it's Elsie, rocking.'

'Oh yes,' said his mum, 'the ghost that you were talking to when I came in before.'

'No,' said Sunny, 'it's not that one, this is another one.'

'I can't keep up,' said his mum, and she went off to sew up some holes.

Sunny's birthday was on the first day of May. This year it fell on a Sunday, and that was the day that was chosen for the trip to the seaside.

On his birthday morning, Sunny opened his presents. There was a magnifying glass, and his dad said, 'I might borrow that off you. I want to see if I can find those ghosts of yours.' And there was a camera as well, an old one that his dad had fixed up.

'As good as new,' said his mum.

'As good as *old*,' said his dad. 'This camera has been taking photographs since your granddad was a baby.'

'I can take it to the seaside with me,' said Sunny. 'Do you think I'll be able to take pictures of the ghosts?' But neither his dad nor his mum seemed to know how to answer this question.

They packed a picnic, and Sunny got out his bucket and spade and a beach cricket set. He brushed his teeth and put on his coat and shoes and picked up his camera. While his dad was looking for his keys, Sunny went out through the shop. As he was going through the front door, he saw his school friend Ellie, who was walking past.

'Hi, Ellie,' said Sunny, holding the shop door open so that Herbert could follow him out.

'Hi, Ellie,' said Herbert.

Ellie's jaw fell open as she stared at Herbert.

Sunny's dad came out behind Herbert, jangling a bunch of keys. 'Are you all right, Ellie?' he said. 'You look as if you've seen a ghost.'

'I . . . uh . . .' said Ellie.

Sunny was still holding the door open, and out came Walter and Violet and Mary and Elsie, each of whom said hello to Sunny's friend. Behind them all came Sunny's mum, who said, 'Thank you, Sunny,' and locked the shop door behind them. She saw Sunny's friend standing there, and she saw the expression on her face. 'Are you all right, Ellie?' she asked.

'Uh . . . I . . .' said Ellie.

While Sunny's dad was in the van checking the directions to the beach, and Sunny's mum was checking that they had everything they needed for the day, Ellie was looking from one ghost to another. 'Wow,' she said to Sunny, 'you really do have ghosts in your shop.'

'Well,' said Sunny, '*usually* we do, but today we're taking them out. We're taking them to the seaside.'

He opened the back of the van, which did not have any furniture in it today, and the ghosts climbed in.

Sunny said to Herbert, 'You won't feel travel sick, will you?'

'I shall be all right,' said Herbert. 'I can look out of the window at the back.'

Sunny got into the front of the van. He sat in between his mum and dad, holding his camera on his lap. 'I'll see you tomorrow!' he called to Ellie, as they set off.

They listened to the golden oldies on the stereo, and Sunny could hear the ghosts singing along in the back. Sunny's parents never seemed to see or hear the ghosts, but Ellie had seen them, and Sunny thought that it might be like how there were certain sounds, certain frequencies, that could only be heard by young people and dogs.

Then Sunny's mum said to Sunny's dad, 'Can you hear something in the back?'

'It's the ghosts,' said Sunny.

'I'm sure I just heard something,' she said to Sunny's dad. 'Didn't you?'

'It's the ghosts,' said Sunny.

'Perhaps it's the wind getting in somewhere,' said Sunny's dad.

'It's the ghosts,' said Sunny.

'Yes,' said Sunny's mum, 'it's probably the wind getting in.'

When they got to the seaside, Sunny went round to the back of the van and opened the doors.

'There's nothing in there, is there?' said his dad, who was already holding the bucket and spade and the beach cricket set and the picnic.

'I'm letting the ghosts out,' said Sunny.

'You can let that wind out as well,' said his dad.

When all five ghosts were out, Sunny shut the van doors, and the eight of them walked along the promenade. Sunny's mum and dad were in front, and the five ghosts followed behind them, and Sunny skipped between them. The ghosts knew a seaside song that Sunny had never heard before. They sang it, and when he had heard the chorus a few times, Sunny joined in:

Oh, I do like to be beside the seaside,
I do like to be beside the sea,
I do like to stroll along the prom, prom, prom,
Where the brass bands play,
'Tiddely-om-pom-pom!'

'I haven't heard that for a very long time,' said his mum.

'The ghosts were singing it,' said Sunny.

'Do the brass bands still play?' asked Mary, looking around.

'Not so much,' said Herbert.

'That is a shame,' said Mary.

They all went down onto the beach. Sunny's parents hired a pair of deckchairs and got comfortable, and Sunny built a sandcastle. When he went looking for pebbles and shells with which to decorate it, Herbert came with him - he turned out to have a very good eye for the best shells. Walter stayed by the sandcastle, guarding it, shooing away a dog that looked like it might knock the sandcastle down. Mary and Elsie walked down to the edge of the sea, where they stood in the shallows, each one holding the hem of her nightie out of the water, even though it seemed unlikely that the ghostly nighties could get wet. Violet sat down on the sand and opened the notepad she was carrying.

'How are you getting on with your book, Violet?' asked Sunny.

'All right, I think,' said Violet.

'What are you writing about?' asked Sunny.

'I'm writing about you,' said Violet.

'About me?' asked Sunny.

'About all of you,' said Violet. She turned her notepad back to the first page and showed him what she had written there: *Sunny and the Ghosts*. 'I've written about you meeting Herbert and Walter, and I've written about you meeting me and the Miss Constantines. I'll need to ask you some questions,' she added, showing him a list she had made. The first question was, *How long has Sunny's family had the shop?* The questions covered two whole pages. The last question was, *Is there any more bubblewrap?*

'Now I'm writing about this,' she said. She turned back to the page on which she had been writing, at the top of which it said, *Walter stayed by the sandcastle, guarding it, shooing away a dog that looked like it might knock the sandcastle down. Mary and Elsie walked down to the edge of the sea . . .*

'After this, we'll need something else to happen, won't we?' she said.

'Yes,' said Sunny, 'I suppose so.'

Violet was scribbling again. Sunny looked and saw that she was writing down the conversation that they had just had.

Sunny's mum called him over for the picnic, and Violet said, 'I'll come and sit with you, so that I can hear what you're all saying.'

Sunny sat down on the picnic blanket, and his mum passed him a plate and said, 'Do the ghosts need plates?'

'No,' said Sunny. 'I don't think ghosts eat.'

'Thank you for thinking of us,' said Violet, looking up from her notepad, 'but no, we don't eat.'

'Glad to hear it,' said Sunny's dad. 'All the more for the rest of us.'

Sunny's mum unpacked the picnic. There were three sorts of sandwiches, as well as eggs, sausages, tomatoes, crisps and strawberries, and after all that there was a birthday cake, with nine candles on top, which would not stay lit long enough for Sunny to blow them out.

'Your ghosts keep blowing them out,' said his dad.

'No,' said Sunny, 'it's just the wind.'

After the picnic, Sunny and his mum and dad set up a game of beach cricket. Herbert tried to join in. He nearly caught the ball – he nearly caught Sunny's dad out – but the ball went straight through his cupped hands and straight through his body. 'I'm going to have to practise my catching,' said Herbert.

Mary and Elsie, who all this time had been standing and talking at the edge of the sea, began to walk back up the beach. Sunny went to meet them, and Mary said, 'Sunny, we would like to thank you for bringing us to the seaside. We've had a lovely time. We've decided to stay here, at least for a while. It has always been a dream of ours to live by the sea.'

'But where will you live?' asked Sunny. 'I mean, you won't stay right here, on the beach, will you?'

The sisters turned and looked at a grand old hotel on the seafront. It had seen better days – some of the letters in the hotel's name had fallen off leaving behind

HO EL
SP END D

– but Mary said, 'I think we might stay there, don't you, Elsie?'

'That looks perfect to me,' said Elsie.

'We'll miss you,' said Sunny.

'We'll miss you too,' said Mary. 'Perhaps you could come and visit.'

'Can I take a photo of you, before you go?' asked Sunny.

'You can try,' said Mary.

All five ghosts gathered together around the sand-castle, and Sunny held the camera's viewfinder up to his eye.

'None of you are smiling,' he said. 'Say cheese!'

The ghosts said, 'Cheese!' and Sunny took the picture.

Then Mary and Elsie said goodbye to Sunny and Herbert and Walter and Violet, and Sunny and Herbert and Walter and Violet said goodbye to Mary and Elsie, and the sisters walked together up the steps onto the promenade and into the Hotel Splendid.

'Time to get back in the van,' called Sunny's dad.

The picnic things had been packed away. Sunny picked up his bucket and spade. 'Come on, then,' he said to the remaining ghosts.

On the way back, he fell asleep, and he was still half asleep when his mum helped him out of the van and into the house, and got him into his pyjamas, and got his teeth brushed, and got him into his bed. When Sunny woke up in the morning and realised that he had come inside and gone to bed without taking care of the ghosts, he ran into his parents' bedroom begging

them to open the front door and the back of the van. 'The ghosts have been locked in the van all night!' he said. 'They won't have been able to get out. They'll be cold and bored and worried.'

'I think they're all right,' said his dad.

'But they can't go through doors,' said Sunny, 'apart from Walter, who finds it very uncomfortable, and can't do it when he's tired.'

'I opened the back of the van when we got home,' said his dad. 'I held it open so that they could climb out. And I held open the door of the shop, so that they could get inside. I thought they would want to be in their own places. In the blanket box, isn't it, and in the wardrobe?'

'But I thought you couldn't see them,' said Sunny. 'I thought you didn't believe in them.'

'Well,' said his dad, 'I can't, and I'm not sure I do, but I can keep an open mind.'

'Thanks, Dad,' said Sunny.

'Now,' said his dad, 'toast or cereal for breakfast?'

CHAPTER FIVE

The Sixth Ghost

A FEW WEEKS later, Sunny's dad came into the kitchen with some post that had just come through the letterbox. 'Who are Mary and Elsie?' he asked.

Sunny, who had been spooning cereal into his mouth, looked up.

'Mary and Elsie?' said his mum. 'I don't know.'

'There's a postcard here,' said Sunny's dad. 'It's addressed to *Everyone*, at the shop's address. It says, *Dear all, We are having a lovely time,* and it's signed, *With love from Mary and Elsie.*' He put the postcard down on the table and Sunny saw the picture on the front: a view of the Hotel Splendid.

'Well, I'm glad they're having a lovely time,' said Sunny's mum, 'whoever they are.'

'Now everyone's happy,' said Sunny, looking around the shop. It was bedtime, but Sunny had come downstairs to look for his camera. Herbert and Walter were sitting by the window, reading in the glow from the streetlamp. They looked very peaceful, like old friends. Violet was sitting at the cash desk, writing her book. Mary and Elsie were at the seaside. 'Everyone's got what they want,' he said.

'Aye,' agreed Walter, turning the page of his book.

'Very happy,' said Violet, dotting an i and crossing a t in her notepad.

But Herbert was quiet, which was very unusual.

'Are you all right, Herbert?' asked Sunny.

Herbert mumbled something sadly, and Sunny had to ask him to say it again.

'I wanted to play the piano,' said Herbert.

'But the piano's gone, Herbert,' said Sunny.

'Why didn't you play it while it was here?' asked Walter.

'I didn't know how,' said Herbert. 'I never learnt.'

'Well then, why didn't you tell me you wanted to learn?' asked Walter. 'You always complained when I played.'

'I was jealous,' admitted Herbert, 'because you played so beautifully and I couldn't play at all.'

'Well I could have shown you how,' said Walter.

'But the piano's gone now,' said Sunny.

Herbert sighed and went back to his book.

'Oh here's my camera,' said Sunny, finding it on the floor, on the rug in front of the leather trunk. He didn't know how it had got there. He picked it up and brought the viewfinder up to his eye, turning to face Violet at the cash desk. 'Smile!' he said.

Violet smiled. 'If my book gets published,' she said, 'perhaps we could use your photo of me on the back cover. Or on my website. I'd like to have a website.'

'That's odd,' said Sunny, inspecting his camera.

'What's odd?' asked Herbert.

'My camera won't take any more pictures,' said Sunny.

'Let's have a look at it,' said Herbert. He had a fiddle with it and then said, 'It's full. You've used up the roll of film.'

'How can it be full?' asked Sunny. 'I've only taken one photo, at the seaside.'

'It's a mystery,' said Herbert.

Sunny's mum sent the film off to be developed. When the packet of photographs came back, she said to Sunny, 'There is a picture of your sandcastle here, but apart from that they're just photos of the shop, not really of anything in particular, just random shots taken at odd angles. You must have been pressing the button by mistake, without realising it.'

Sunny spread the photographs out on the kitchen table. One was of the sandcastle and all the ghosts. All the rest, taken inside the shop, were pictures of a ghost he had never seen before. The ghost in these photographs was pulling faces and sticking out his ghostly tongue.

'Isn't it strange?' said his mum.

'Yes,' said Sunny, who had no idea who this ghost was. 'It's very strange.'

He took the photographs down to the shop and showed them to Herbert and Walter and Violet.

'Do any of you know who this ghost is?' asked Sunny.

'No,' said Herbert.

'No,' said Walter.

'No,' said Violet, 'but I have seen him.'

'You've seen him?' asked Sunny.

'Yes,' said Violet. 'I saw him in the stationery cupboard. He pulled my hair. I don't know who he is though.'

Sunny stood thinking and looking around the shop, and in the silence he heard a popping sound. *Pop-pop-pop.* He took a step in the direction of the popping

sound, moving towards the leather trunk. *Pop-pop-pop*. He lifted the lid of the trunk. *Pop-pop-pop*. And there was a ghost, wearing a silk dressing gown and a monocle. It was the ghost that had been pulling faces and sticking out his ghostly tongue in the photographs. Now he was popping bubblewrap.

'Who are you?' asked Sunny.

'My name,' said the ghost, 'is Peregrine.'

'But what are you doing in here?' asked Sunny.

'I'm popping bubblewrap,' said Peregrine.

'But,' said Sunny, 'what are you *doing* here?'

'Whatever I like,' said Peregrine.

'I mean,' said Sunny, 'I didn't know you were here. How long have you been here?'

'Well,' said Peregrine, 'I was here when the clocks were all telling the wrong time. I was here when the shop was overrun with cats. I was here when the books that you had so carefully shelved ended up scattered all over the place. And I was here when the ugly ornamental pig went missing, and when it got broken.'

'It was you!' said Sunny. 'You changed the time on the clocks, and you brought in all the cats, and you scattered the books, and you broke the pig, and you took my camera without asking and used up all the film . . .'

'I have been busy,' said Peregrine.

'Well it's not very nice of you, is it?' said Sunny.

'No,' said Peregrine, looking pleased. 'It's not very nice, is it? It's very not nice.'

'Apart from the cats,' said Sunny. 'I liked the cats.'

Peregrine looked annoyed.

'Why did you do it all?' asked Sunny.

Peregrine shrugged. 'I was *very nice* and *very good* my whole life,' he said. 'I wanted to be naughty for a change. I want some excitement. I want to run amok.'

And so he did. Sunny was in the shop when, through the front window, he saw Mr Ramsbottom approaching, and then he saw Peregrine, who was standing outside, by the front door, lying in wait. 'Uh-oh,' said Sunny.

Just as Mr Ramsbottom reached for the door handle, Peregrine lifted Mr Ramsbottom's hat off his head and hurled it down the street. Mr Ramsbottom went running after it, and Peregrine watched him with a smirk on his face. When Mr Ramsbottom got back with his hat and came into the shop, he said, 'The wind just blew the hat right off my head.' He turned around to look outside – he didn't seem to notice Peregrine skulking into the shop behind him – and said, 'The funny thing is, it doesn't seem to be in the slightest bit windy today.'

The following morning, Sunny's mum went down to the shop and found Sunny's paint – the paint that was kept in the stationery cupboard – daubed on the walls and dribbled across the floorboards. 'Sunny . . .' she called up the stairs, 'have you had your paints out?'

Sunny knew, as soon as he saw the mess, that Peregrine had done it. When Sunny said, 'It wasn't me!' his mum seemed to believe him, but although she listened to his explanation, she did not really believe in Peregrine.

The paint on the floor made a trail that went from one end of the shop to the other. It went around the silk rug and led, they discovered, to a broken window.

Sunny's mum called the police, who sent someone round to look for fingerprints. There were lots of fingerprints in the shop, of course, because of all the people who came in and looked around and picked things up and put them down again. But the only prints on the pots of paint turned out to be Sunny's.

A police officer sat down with the three of them. She looked long and hard at Sunny and said that the evidence pointed towards this being an inside job. 'Yes,' said Sunny. 'I think it was one of the ghosts, but

the thing is, I don't think ghosts have fingerprints.'
The police officer raised her eyebrows.

Sunny helped his mum and dad clean up, and his
dad said that it was all very strange, and his mum said
that it was a mystery, as she wiped a streak of stray
paint off the side of the leather trunk.

On Saturday, Sunny turned the shop door sign
around so that instead of saying CLOSED it said
OPEN, or at least that's what Sunny thought.

It was a very quiet morning, during which a
number of people came to the door but then went
away again without coming inside. In the middle
of the day, Sunny's mum went outside to water the
hanging baskets, and as she came back into the shop,
she stopped and looked at the sign on the door.

'Come and look at this,' she said to Sunny, who
went over and saw that the OPEN side of the sign
now said:

CLOSED
~~OPEN~~
~~Monday to Saturday~~
~~9am to 5pm~~
Go AWAY

'I think I know who did that,' said Sunny.

'I think I know what you're going to say,' said his mum.

And they both said together, 'Peregrine.'

Peregrine also bothered the other ghosts. When Herbert and Walter were trying to read, Peregrine poked them and made annoying noises in their ears. When Violet was trying to write, Peregrine knocked the pen out of her hand.

Violet tried being friendly and talking to him but he was just rude to her. When she asked him whether he liked the shop, he said, 'No, it's a stupid shop, full of junk.' When she asked him why he'd avoided meeting everyone for so long, he said, 'You all sounded so stupid and boring, why on earth would I want to meet you?'

She asked him what he missed most about life. 'Herbert misses gobstoppers,' she said.

'I don't miss anything,' said Peregrine. 'I'm having much more fun now.'

All night long, Peregrine went about making a nuisance of himself, and at dawn he got back inside his leather trunk to rest and think of more not-nice things and more not-good things to do.

Herbert and Walter were complaining to Sunny about Peregrine when the shop door opened and Mr Ramsbottom came in, holding his hat onto his head with his hand. Sunny's dad was behind the cash desk, and Mr Ramsbottom said to him, 'I want my money back for that piano.'

'Oh,' said Sunny's dad. 'What seems to be the problem?'

'I'm going to join my sister in New York,' said Mr Ramsbottom, 'and I'm not taking the piano with me.'

Sunny's dad sighed. 'All right,' he said. 'We'll come and fetch the piano and give you your money back.'

Mr Ramsbottom nodded. 'Good,' he said. 'And she's changed her mind about the books – she wants them back.' He wandered over to the bookcase and looked at the books displayed on the shelves. 'You'd better sort them out, pack them up.'

He looked at the pigs that were now living on top of the bookcase: the unbroken pig, the carefully mended pig, and a new pig that someone had brought in, so now there were three of them. Mr Ramsbottom picked up the unbroken pig, which was so fat, so round, that it fitted his hand as neatly as one of the plastic apples, though it was heavier, and more fragile. He picked up the carefully mended pig. Now he had one in each hand, like two juggling balls.

Sunny's dad said, 'Mr Ramsbottom . . .'

Mr Ramsbottom tossed the unbroken pig into the air. When it came down, he caught it.

Sunny said, 'Mr Ramsbottom . . .'

'Stop fretting,' said Mr Ramsbottom. He tossed up the unbroken pig again, and then tossed up the carefully mended one as well, before catching them both. 'I've been practising,' he said. 'I can juggle just about anything.' Still holding the two pigs, he reached for the third pig, the new pig.

Sunny and his dad said together, 'Mr Ramsbottom!'

'Don't put me off,' said Mr Ramsbottom, throwing up the first pig, and the second pig, and the third pig.

Sunny's dad took a step towards Mr Ramsbottom, who – trying now to keep track of three pigs, to catch all three with only two hands – fumbled. Sunny and his dad watched the pigs fall to the ground, where they smashed.

'You put me off,' said Mr Ramsbottom.

The three of them looked down at the smashed pigs. Mr Ramsbottom moved away from the breakage.

Sunny's dad said, 'When are you leaving for New York, Mr Ramsbottom?'

'As soon as possible,' he replied. 'When are you going to come and fetch that piano of yours?'

Sunny's dad agreed a day and a time with Mr Ramsbottom.

'And what about the books?' said Mr Ramsbottom. 'How are you going to get them to New York?'

Sunny looked at the books. He thought of them going all the way to America, and he had an idea. 'Perhaps,' he said, 'Mr Ramsbottom's books could be put in the leather trunk.' He pointed to Peregrine's trunk. 'We could ship the trunk to New York for you, Mr Ramsbottom.'

'Hm,' said Mr Ramsbottom, eyeing the handsome trunk.

'The only thing is,' said Sunny, 'it comes with a ghost.'

'Nonsense,' said Mr Ramsbottom. 'I don't believe in ghosts.'

'Shall we put your books in the trunk then, Mr Ramsbottom,' said Sunny, 'and send it to New York?'

Mr Ramsbottom was looking at the price tag on the trunk. 'So you give me back my money for the piano,' he said, 'minus the cost of the books and the trunk . . .'

'. . . and the pigs,' said Sunny's dad, doing a quick sum on a scrap of paper, 'and I'd say that makes us even.'

Mr Ramsbottom grumbled about the pigs, but in the end he said, 'All right, that's what we'll do.'

So that's what they did. During the night – while Peregrine was in the garden pulling the heads off the flowers, pulling plants up by their roots, and stamping on the food that had been put out for the birds and the hedgehogs – Herbert, Walter and Violet were busy in the shop, taking the books out of the bookcase and putting them into the leather trunk. They found *A Christmas Carol* in there already. There was plenty of space in the trunk for all the books and for Peregrine. He was always tired after misbehaving and, when he came in from the garden, he climbed back inside his trunk. He grouched about the books that were in there, but he settled down on top of them and closed the lid. Meanwhile, Sunny's dad was finishing his breakfast. When he came down to the shop, he labelled the trunk, and by the time he had done that a man with a van was at the door ready to collect it.

Sunny, Herbert, Walter and Violet gathered at the front of the shop to watch as Peregrine's trunk was put into the back of the van.

'He did say he wanted some excitement,' said Violet, as the trunk began its three-thousand-mile journey to Mr Ramsbottom's new home in New York.

'Those two were made for each other,' said Walter.

As the van accelerated up the road, Violet blew a raspberry and Sunny tried to high-five Herbert. When the van had disappeared around the corner, Sunny led the ghosts in a conga; they congaed back into the shop and Sunny's dad closed the door behind them.

Epilogue

'BUT WHAT WILL I do now,' said Herbert, 'without the books to read?'

'Well,' said Walter, 'we've got the piano back, haven't we?' He wandered over to the piano which had been returned to what had been a long, bare space in its absence. 'Now I can teach you how to play.'

During the night, in the weeks that followed, if Sunny woke, or perhaps in his dreams, he was likely to hear Herbert practising his scales, or Walter playing a tune and then Herbert trying it, and he heard *Bananas in Pyjamas* about a hundred or a thousand or a hundred thousand times, but he didn't mind.

Violet liked to hear the music too, while she sat through the dark hours, scribbling away.

At other times, it was quiet, because they did have books as well – Sunny's dad had come up from the cellar with another boxful, saying, 'Right, we've got

room on the shelves for this lot now.' ('My books!' said Violet when she saw them.)

And new things came in all the time – or rather, old things. Someone brought in a spare piano stool, and Herbert and Walter played duets. Someone else came in with an old writing desk, which they no longer wanted but which Violet loved and made good use of. There were more clocks, more framed butterflies, more ornamental animals, and one day another wardrobe arrived in the shop. It was fancier than the other one; it had curlicues and a mirrored door. Sunny, watching this piece of furniture being lugged through the front door, wondered whether there was really room in the shop for a second wardrobe. By moving things around, though, space was made next to Walter's wardrobe, and that's where the second wardrobe went. Sunny whistled while he polished it, and then he opened the wardrobe door and looked inside.

'Dad,' he said, 'there's a ghost in here.'

'What a surprise,' said his dad.

Welcome to my website!

Name:	Violet van Bruggen
Occupation:	Ghost writer
Hair:	Frizzy
Eyes:	See-through
Born:	January 1971
Died:	Yes
Favourite colour:	Turquoise

Resides:	In an antiques shop in Devon with my friends. I divide my time between the stationery cupboard (daytime) and my writing desk (nighttime).
Likes:	Writing stories, getting ideas for more stories, listening to people's conversations, popping bubble-wrap.
Dislikes:	Being walked through, having my hair pulled, having the pen knocked out of my hand when I'm trying to write, finding the bubble-wrap already popped, electrical appliances.
Top tip:	If you've got an idea for a story, get writing! Don't let little worries – like *But it might not be any good* or *But I'm dead now* – get in your way. Just start, and see what happens next.

Coming soon!

Sunny and the Hotel Splendid

On the hottest day of the year, Ana Sharma and her mum check in to the Hotel Splendid, a place where bells seem to ring all by themselves, jam pots and milk jugs appear on the breakfast table as if by magic, and things go bump in the night. The Hotel Splendid has a problem. When Ana and Sunny meet, they come up with a solution, but one problem leads to another. Meanwhile, the hotel is harbouring an unexpected guest . . .

This book has been typeset by
SALT PUBLISHING LIMITED
using Neacademia, a font designed by Sergei Egorov
for the Rosetta Type Foundry in the Czech Republic. It
is manufactured using Holmen Book Cream 70gsm, a
Forest Stewardship Council™ certified paper from the
Hallsta Paper Mill in Sweden. It was printed and bound
by Clays Limited in Bungay, Suffolk, Great Britain.

CROMER
GREAT BRITAIN
MMXVIII